Z

The wish

I saw a star fall from the sky
I closed my eyes to wish
A moment of quiet, eyes shut tight
A time not to be missed

I wished for peace and happiness
For all who walked the earth
Hungry tummies to be full
Children to laugh with mirth

The pain to stop for prisoners
Locked in a foreign land
But most of all I wished that
Humans could love and understand.

ZodoFF

For Sandra

ZodoFF

Cloudy Day Books
USA. Portugal...London. Aberdeen

ISBN 978-1-4092-5640-3

1ˢᵗ Printing June 2009.
www.juliehodgson.com
www.cloudydaybooks.com
http://www.shamrockediting.blogspot.com
Cover art work by Luca Oleastri

"Maxima debetur puero reverential."

"We owe the greatest respect to a child."

"Fear less, hope more;
Whine less, breathe more;
Talk less, say more;
Hate less, love more;
And all good things are yours."

Swedish proverb

ZodoFF

Table of Contents

You ready then?

Chapter One

Blueberries Oh Blueberries

"Now, stop THAT!" screamed Lucy at the top of her voice which echoed around the forest.

Jerry just laughed and kicked the huge pine cones hard against the tree. They ricocheted against the branches and shot past Lucy's nose...just missing her.

Geesh! Jerry could be a pain at times. He was sometimes the dumbest big brother that ever set foot on this earth! Lucy thought. What was Mum thinking of when she said it was okay for Jerry to keep an eye on her when they walked through Crag Bank Forest to get back home? The forest was dense with shrubs and trees, tall pine trees stretching up to the heavens and a great place for mushroom and blueberry picking. They often came down here to walk through the forest. Usually getting blue lips from all the blueberries they scoffed along the way. Jerry started singing "blue mooooon" and making an O shape with his mouth as he did it. Mouth crammed with berries. Laughing as the blue juice dripped down his chin. Lucy just smiled at her stupid, blue-lipped big brother and carried on walking.

On this particular morning, the rain had fallen earlier and the forest had that fantastic smell of damp moss and mushrooms.

The mist rose like a spectre rising from the mossy beds stretching its arms as it went up into the sky forcing its way through the thick trees. The sun tried to stream through the tall trees as best as it could. It beamed like golden knives penetrating through the clouds, stabbing the trees with intermittent shadows piercing the light like a laser show from heaven.

Lucy had collected quite a few autumn mushrooms and other ones, that were golden and shaped like tiny fingers, lay in her basket. Jerry had thrown blueberries at her and her face was also now blue. Although…in her favour…Jerry's face got its fair share of the little blue bombs during their blueberry battle. He did, in fact, look worse than she did.

Jerry was now scuffing his trainers through the damp spongy moss, getting a bit bored with pine cone kicking.

"Luce, lets go deeper into the forest and explore a little."

"Hmmm, you know what Mum said, no mischief because if the WE.C.U group hear of this unauthorised outing we'll get it for sure," sighed Lucy

"Ah Lucy, don't be daft. It's cool and it's not that far and anyway, we can get a whole load of mushrooms for Mum to dry," persuaded Jerry with his lop-sided smile.

Lucy was all up for an adventure, NOT for getting grounded by her parents, but in reality, it was the authorities that were the thorns in their sides, not their parents. But they still had to be careful.

They decided to tramp off further into the forest, but not so far that it would take them more than 15 minutes to get back to the edge of the forest to the field that connected to the back of their house.

"Over here!" shouted Lucy.

"More mushrooms by this tree," she said as she bent down and picked up the biggest puffball mushroom and placed it carefully into her basket…smiling because she had got the biggest one so far today.

Jerry raised his eyebrows at the size of the mushroom without uttering a syllable, then scurried off ahead to find an even bigger one, half laughing to himself.

They had spent quite some time picking mushrooms and flicking blueberries at each other and had wandered onto a path into a clearing they had never noticed before.

They looked at each other, shrugged their shoulders and started to walk the path; just a dirt path, but a distinctive path at that.

As they walked about 10 steps in, the beautiful greens of the trees and the blues of the skies gradually changed to black and white;

everything from the golden shafts of sunlight turned silver instead. It was as if they were in one of their Nanna Rawes' old fashioned black and white photographs that she used to show them.

They were so shocked they raced back to the beginning of the path just to "feel" the colours again.

"What on earth was that?" They asked each other in unison.

They didn't know whether to be scared or to laugh. But they were both adventurers at heart and made the steps forward. Jerry had his new 15.1 mega pixel digital camera with him that he had got for Christmas. He took photograph after photograph, while walking, not really looking at what he was taking; he just took them. If he got caught using the camera outdoors, that would be another matter!

It was only a matter of 30 seconds before the forest went black and white again. They stood stock still for a moment when it happened, so still, hardly daring to breathe, their heartbeats thumping in their chests.

"Wow, now this is SO cool," whispered Jerry. Why he whispered is anyone's guess. He cocked his head to one side to see if it would all change.

"Hmm." Lucy was looking off to her left, where she pointed to smoke rising up from the distance.

There was also a strange glow up in the air above the forest.

Jerry said, "Let's go and investigate, but we can keep to a distance." He was still in awe of the changes. Even the red forest squirrel was not "in colour" any more. Even their clothes were the dull colours of an old black and white television show. Quite comical really, but the burning question on both of their minds was why?

London Reuters. New law passed 2708 section 5 under no circumstances must any photograph of a child be shown in public. Even if taken in the privacy of their own home. "For the good of the child" informs Minister. All photographic centres will now be monitored by the WE.C.U group.

Chapter 2

Unexpected Events

The sky was clear and the sun was shining silver strands through the trees, like giant swords slicing through the air. Jerry and Lucy veered off the path they were on and followed the plume of smoke. Lucy spotted an old fence beside a lake.

"What on earth is a lake doing here in the middle of the forest?" Lucy mumbled half to herself but wanting Jerry to hear. It probably wasn't even on the Ordinance Survey Map their parents had; Lucy would bet on it. The fence was half buried with moss and old branches intertwined through the holes in the wood. It looked like it was being pulled under the earth slowly.

The lake was a glittering glass bowl. It had a small rowing boat moored to a very rusty pole bobbing in the water.

Lucy sighed and said, "Wow, if there had been a tiny bridge over that lake we could have played pooh sticks. Even though it's a prohibited game, we could have snuck in a race or two." Lucy always played piglet and so loved playing.

They were so engrossed in their fascination of their new surroundings; they did not see the old man walk up behind them with a stick in his hand.

"Oy what's all this 'ere then?" he asked in a gruff voice.

Poor Lucy and Jerry nearly jumped out of their skins with fright.

They spun round on their heels to face a scruffy, dishevelled old man with a big, bushy beard and old fashioned flat cap on his head, wearing denim jeans and a lumberjack shirt. Of course, still everything was in black and white. But strangely, he had the bluest eyes they had ever seen, which shone, and the depth of colour was mesmerising and surreal to look at, but it was very hard *not* to look at them.

"S…S…S…Sorry, we were lost," stuttered Jerry, knowing that probably got them out of a spot of bother.

The old man looked at the two children in front of him and with a wry smile, held out his hand and said,

"Well, in that case, pleased to meet you both. Joe's the name, *just Joe*." He turned the two around so their backs faced the forest.

"Lucy," she said, holding out her hand.

"Jerry, Lucy's older brother," he smiled, holding out his hand too.

"So what are you doing here then?" said Joe.

"We are just mushroom and blueberry picking, that's all, as we do most autumns."

"But ere, my place I mean, how did ya find it? Ain't seen anyone 'ere for many sunrises."

"Well, we've no idea really, we just followed the smoke signals from your camp fire," Jerry said smiling to himself.

They stood beside each other, strange old man and two children in a forest clearing, with a lake that didn't fit in the forest and everything looking like an old black and white movie. The moss on the ground, which was perfect for mushroom picking, had no mushrooms on it, let alone anything else, just their damp footprints. It felt like their feet were sinking into the moist ground.

Lucy wandered off towards the lake, not wanting to be confused anymore. As she got near the bank, the water seemed to disappear. She went to shout back to Jerry but couldn't move, let alone shout to him. Terrified, she fought the feeling of your mind being awake and your body being totally paralysed and no matter what you did or how much you tried to move you couldn't.

Jerry was chatting away, just small talk with Joe, and glanced over at Lucy who stood perfectly still staring at the lake. He wondered what she had seen; but not wanting to be rude towards Joe, he kept listening to the old man's ramblings. It was as if he hadn't seen or spoke to anyone in years, just like he had said.

After a few seconds, he shouted, "Luce!" but he got nothing back. "LUCE!" Again, no response.

He was getting annoyed that she was probably playing deaf on him more than anything else. *Why wasn't she turning around? Was it to be cheeky to him like she usually does?*

By now Lucy was panicking, sweating, tears streaming down her face, her heart thumping in her chest, her legs feeling like jelly.

Jerry walked towards Lucy and had gotten just a couple of steps from her when Joe called him back to see the big fish he had caught in the lake that very morning, thus distracting Jerry once again, leaving Lucy paralysed and terrified. The lake was no more in her vision; the trees had melded themselves and looked like the most horrible creatures. *Was it her imagination or a reality? Who knew?* She was just terrified and so desperate for Jerry to come. She was fighting the gut-wrenching fear with all her might.

By this time, Jerry's being polite and looking at big fish had got boring; he was getting concerned about Lucy's lack of cheek towards him. It was weird.

He finally left Joe, rambling on to himself about how this fish just jumped on to his lure, etc. He strode off into Lucy's direction and went to grab her by the shoulders. As he did so he stood right in front of her; blocking her vision of the lake, he noticed her standing stock still, tears streaming down her face.

In the instance of him blocking her vision, she immediately came out of the trance, shaking uncontrollably. She fell into his arms, her voice coming through racking sobs.

"Don't look at the lake," she gasped.

"Calm down, Luce, what's wrong?" He asked as he took her closer, soothing her hair.

Lucy related to Jerry what had happened and Jerry knew Lucy would never tell a lie, especially about things like this; the emotion was too real. (She was a real goody two shoes in the making.)

He didn't turn and look at the lake as he consoled her. He moved her away from the edge and walked her back towards where the old gate was buried half way into the moss.

Joe, in the meantime, was still mumbling away to himself as if Jerry was still there; he really looked as if he was talking to someone. He didn't even seem to notice them missing; he was in another world. A world far away from where the two children stood now.

Jerry did his best to calm Lucy down and to resist the strong urge to turn round and look at the lake.

Jerry suggested they get out of the area fast and they made their way back home. Clearly, Lucy was still upset. Scared at what had happened, she still shivered and held onto Jerry's jacket, a rare moment of sibling closeness without the rivalry. She stared at her shoes in an effort to avert her eyes from the lake or anything that might take her back to where she had been only a few moments ago. Time is a strange thing; when you're in trouble, time is slow; when having fun, it whizzes past your nose so fast you hardly see it.

They made their way to the edge of the clearing and walked towards the pathway until everything changed back to its normal colour. They were both looking forward to getting home; the main reason was it was nearly tea time and their Mum was making Toad in the Hole and they loved that. Their Mum was great in the kitchen, baked all the time so a steady stream of cakes and buns were always available. Dad, on the other hand, just baked bread on Saturday mornings. Fantastic it was too, and so soft and smelled great when it was first out of the oven. They had very normal parents in this very abnormal world in which they lived.

USA. CNN. Reports. New law passed 2708, section 7 if a child falls over on a playground and hurts themselves only the designated teacher may help. Although no tactile contact must be used. (Regardless of anyone else in the immediate vicinity.) Parents are strictly forbidden to enter the playground until the bell rings. Whether playground supervisors are there or not. All incidents must be reported. This is for "the good of the child" All carnival floats have been banned for health and safety reasons. Says Intern in Washington.

Chapter 3

The Plan Runs its Course

Lucy was quiet all the way home; Jerry in his big brother way thought how peaceful it was and smiled to himself. He walked with his arm round her shoulders to protect her. The blueberries and mushrooms forgotten, they would collect them another day, when Luce was up to it. They would have to get the basket back anyway, but couldn't even remember where Lucy, or he for that matter, had laid it down. That's another problem for another day.

Once home, Lucy went to her room while Jerry explained to their Mum that Lucy didn't feel well and it was probably caused by eating too many blueberries.

Jerry went on his Xbox and started racing with a friend online. While his car veered around the tight street bends of the game, he thought about what had happened. *They must return, possibly with their cousin Frank, who was 16, and very level headed for his age and who would surely help. Jerry would send him an e-mail later…of course, carefully worded as all internet activity was monitored by the WE.C.U group.* But he was desperate to win this game against his friend. Tea was ready; he could smell the aroma of his Mum's Toad in the Hole drift up the stairs, enough to make anyone move from a game or a computer screen very rapidly indeed. He walked past Lucy's room to see her seated by her desk, drawing in her sketch pad.

"You okay, Luce?"

"Yea, just drawing what I saw at the lake so you could understand what I meant by what I was trying to explain to you back there."

He leaned in over her shoulder and saw the drawing she had made; he shuddered when he saw the trees formed as horrific images, intertwined with hellish, screaming faces.

"Wow, Luce, you must have been really scared." He ruffled her hair and raced downstairs for tea.

She ran after him, pushing him out the way to get to the table first. He was glad she did that, actually, as it meant she was coming back to her old self.

During tea, neither of them mentioned what had happened to them, as they knew their Mum would just worry and not let them back, so they explained that they forgot the basket and would return the next day to fetch it. It wasn't a problem as far as she was concerned and she didn't say anything to the contrary.

"Luce, we will go tomorrow again; shall I ask Frank to come with us?" He whispered when his Mum went into the kitchen to fetch the rice pudding out of the oven.

"Yup, the more the better and we can trust Frank. Are you going to ring him?" Lucy asked him.

"After the rice pudding," he said. "I'm not missing that. And I have e-mailed him but it's worded in code so that the nosy parkers don't understand it. A phone call as well is a must, I guess, at least to explain it properly." He smiled at his little sis then walked over to his Mum.

Jerry immediately asked to use the phone and settled into a conversation with Frank. Lucy went upstairs to her laptop and went online to do some research for a school project she was doing on 17th century history in London. She had already made some rubbings from an old church, which she had put into plastic folders ready for her presentation in two weeks time. She read the list of words she was allowed to use and the ones that had been banned from the English language by the WE.C.U group and carefully wrote them into her project notes. *How on earth she was going to explain the Black Death in her other assignment was anybody's guess! Maybe call it the dark death?* She frowned. It was difficult to learn things when so much was prohibited. She had wanted to write about Irene Sendler, a Polish Catholic who saved thousands of Jewish children in the holocaust. She kept all the names of the children she saved in a jam jar. But it wasn't allowed in the curriculum, and many said it never even happened. But Lucy knew better. Her grandfather had many stories to tell and she had loved listening to him. But all the tales told were in absolute secrecy of course, and in this world of ageism, her grandfather gave up trying to tell others of the world events that had passed. He never got any respect off anyone other than his family. But after all, he was young once; all his hopes and dreams were always there just like in a young person. Just the skin was different; he was still *HIM* inside. Lucy sometimes felt like Anne Frank and had started a diary in a similar way; but was just writing her thoughts about this world of "everything prohibited, nothing allowed, blah blah blah."

"Luce." Jerry smiled.

"Tomorrow we meet Frank early, 8am okay?"

"Do I have a choice?" Lucy sighed.

"You don't have to come if you really don't want to."

"No, I'll come, it's the least I can do; anyway we need to look for the basket. I can't remember where I put it down, can you?"

"Nope," he smiled at his little sister. "Look Luce, you will be fine, we will look out for you, ok?"

"I suppose so," she knowingly smiled back...

"Let's get our heads down; eh, sis, then tomorrow is another day. Adventure is on the edge of our memories at the moment; no telling what will happen, but rest assured, we will stick together and Frank and I will be by your side." He ruffled her hair and headed upstairs.

Jerry was up early and had made some sandwiches and a flask of tea. His Mum knew they were all going off for the day for a picnic and more berry picking. Frank rode his bike to the back porch and knocked quietly.

"You up then, where's Luce?" Frank laughed as he walked through the back door.

Lucy appeared at the bottom of the stairs, rubbing the sleep out of her eyes. She had bad dreams during the night and wasn't looking forward to this at all.

"It will be fine Luce; we are here, so stop worrying. Frank has a brilliant idea; tell her Frank."

"Well I have a pocket mirror with me and we can look at the lake without actually looking at it, if you get my meaning." Frank spun round holding the mirror to his shoulder and looked through it to show her. Lucy was impressed and felt slightly better than before. She walked to the kitchen cupboards and grabbed some cereal for her breakfast. She would need all the strength she could muster. Frank and Jerry sat on the kitchen work tops swinging their feet, waiting for Lucy to finish. Jerry had already eaten four pieces of peanut butter on toast and was raring to go.

"We won't bike it, eh, Frank? Just walk because if we have to run it will be better without the bikes," Jerry laughed to try and lighten the mood of Lucy.

Lucy finished off her breakfast, drank some orange juice, then went upstairs, cleaned her teeth, grabbed her coat and jumped down the stairs two at a time. The three set off through the back of the house, through the field that adjoined the garden. Once they were at the edge of the forest Jerry got his digital camera ready again; he had shown the photos of the world turning black and white to Frank, who thought it was awesome.

They trudged through the paths, Frank playing at kicking cones to Jerry as they walked on. The path was in view now and Jerry just pointed and shouted "Ta da!"

"Is that it then?" Frank chuckled, "Doesn't look very scary."

"Just hold your horses matey; we need to walk down the pathway yet, and keep an eye on the colour changing…it's so weird."

Frank laughed and started talking in a ministerial voice… "Eh guess what I heard? There's a new EU Directive No. 555231" he paused for effect…

"In order to meet the conditions for joining the Single European currency, all citizens of the United Kingdom of Great Britain and Northern Ireland must be made aware that the phrase 'Spending a Penny' is not to be used after 31st December, 2015."

Frank was laughing as he said it.

"From this date, the correct terminology will be: '*Euronating*'." He was giggling.

"Thank you for your co-operation," Frank, now laughing and crying at the same time, bowed to his audience.

Lucy just stood to the right of them with her hands placed on her hips, watching the two young lads mess about pushing each other along the start of the pathway, Frank telling his stupid jokes. She sighed and rolled her eyes at them. They just laughed and continued messing around. What she didn't know was that the boys had chatted last night and were going to make sure Lucy didn't feel any fear today.

The three of them walked down the pathway, the same route as they had taken before. This time Lucy was slightly in the background of the boys.

As they got further in, the change of colour crept up on them.

"Wow, just the same as Nanna Rawes' black and white photos, just like you said, Jerry." Frank laughed and spun round looking in every direction at the light shafts streaming down from the trees. Silver strips cascaded to the leafy ground.

"Come on, let's get further in," urged Jerry.

The three of them trudged through the pathway, Lucy slightly behind the two boys. It didn't take long before the plume of smoke was spotted by Jerry.

"Right, follow me, you two," he laughed and headed off towards the smoke plumes.

Lucy's mind was racing and the thoughts pulsating through it were frightening her. Not to look at the lake was foremost in her thoughts but, how do you not look at something that's right in front of your nose?

The smoke plumes got closer and closer; Frank and Jerry were still messing around like numpties and Lucy just tried to control the surge of butterflies in her stomach.

As they walked across the clearing towards the broken gate, the old man came toward them.

"Well! Look 'ere who it is then, mind you I've not seen anyone for a long time, so just the *three* of you then?" Just Joe went on and on, holding a fish in his hand to show them, talking like he had not seen anyone for years and years.

"Look at this then; this is what I caught just afore you came, big ain't it?"

He still looked the same; the three of them watched in amazement at him holding this smelly fish at arm's length, toothless grin spread across his face. Frank's jaw dropped when he looked around at everything in black and white; then he spotted the lake in the distance. Jerry had told him not to wander off and not to go near the lake.

With all this going on they did not notice another pair of searing blue eyes in the distance watching them, waiting in the shadows of the trees. Jerry and Frank sauntered off to scout around and look for the mushroom basket, wondering if there were any left in it.

From behind the shadows, a hand stretched out and clasped onto Lucy's mouth; the other arm pulled her into the shadows before Lucy could utter one word.

Austria. October 2015 *more children have been found enslaved in underground bunkers for most of their young lives. A district council man has said that he would investigate this immediately.*

ZodoFF

No one, of course, has been held responsible, and all deny taking part in ignoring the children's cry for help for fear of interfering in others lives...

Chapter 4

It's not what it seems!

Frank was agog at this guy walking around, smiling through black teeth, smelling of fish and chatting about fish, and holding a fish! And telling them where they could get fish from. Fish, fish, fish, that's all he talked about.

Deep in the recesses of Lucy's mind crept a fear she had not felt for a long time. Since her Nanna had passed away, anyway. But the strange thing was that the hand that was held over her mouth was not hostile, but gentle like a Mum would do to gently quiet a child. The creature behind her did not move but shifted position and started to gently pull Lucy back towards the forest. Deeper they went until they came to a clearing. The creature let go of Lucy's mouth but she was unable to utter a word; she glanced at the huge space ship that was parked in the space between the large oak trees in the forest. The hatch was open and strange creatures came out smiling...*well at least she thought they were, nothing about them was angry or bad and she felt comfortable with them.* She smiled to herself as they reminded her of the Smurfs but taller! Blue bodies they had, and the kindest faces she had ever seen. Like her great aunty Elsie's face, kind and smiley. A crew of blue!

They gestured for Lucy to follow them into the ship. She got slightly panicky at the thought, but a voice sounded in her head.

"Do not worry, child of the earth, we mean you no harm."

Lucy took steps up the ramp that shone before her. Golden lights surrounded the ledge on each side; the ship was spherical and beautiful, silver coloured and shiny as the stars. There was a strange hum emitting from the engine too and she heard singing inside the ship, which was soothing and made her want to climb the ramp and see what it was.

The air was as still as a summer's day, but not hot or cold; *just right,* she thought.

As she entered the hull of the ship, she could not believe her eyes, and ears for that matter, as the ship's insides looked just like one of her dreams that she kept having. It was a scene from her Nanna's living room, with an old radio playing in the background, just like her Nanna had. The same song was playing, "when a nightingale sang in Berkley square"...and over in the corner was an old chair and in it sat Santa smiling warmly at her...

"W...W...What? How?!" was all she could say.

The creatures spoke no words with their mouths, but she heard them say to her.

"This is your world, my child; this is your dream; each child that enters this ship has a different view in here and yes you can sit on Santa's knee and ask for anything your little heart desires. If you look out at each of the windows you will see other children's dreams. This is where they are kept, as when you grow up, children of this earth stop dreaming and stop believing in things that are of importance to the earth child. Things are getting worse on this earth and your people that are in charge of the countries you live

in want more and more control of who and what you are. They spend money intended for food on useless killing machines. Control is their main aim."

"Children will soon be taught how to fill in special forms and will have no choice in the matter; these forms will be compulsory and will force children to give details of their parents; what they do and believe in, what they eat, how they care for you as a child...this gives the people who rule these countries total control over you. This control will make the children not hesitate to write anything against the parents, whether it is right or wrong, the innocence will be used against the child to make an insidious plot against the parents. This will be made in the name of "for the good of the child." This, my precious child, is NOT what this is; we are here to rescue the earth children and take the earth to task before it's too late. If the plan does not work, we shall evacuate the earth of all bad people and protect the good ones while we deal with the bad."

"This happened once before in 1939 to 1945 in one of your European countries called Germany. Books were burnt, control was in force, mass murder ensued; forms had to be filled in

telling the leaders exactly what you did, what you believed in, etc. This meant they had total control and could use the information in any way they wished. Also, in America in the 1950's people were labelled and accused of things they had not done, all in the name of justice. Many places all over this earth of yours have imprisoned, accused innocents of witchcraft, enslaved, kidnapped, and tortured people. Many other horrible things man has done to each other are always done in the name of 'one thing or another.' Children are the silent sufferers."

"This is no longer the proper environment for children. Throughout the history of mankind the human beings have squandered the life they have been given and fought for anything that is not theirs, fighting over the most silly things such as a scrap of land or a title or some sort of military honour, blowing each other up and why? But the simple truth is this earth does not belong to the humans; they are only borrowing it and making a terrible mess of it too. We have a saying on our planet, 'If you abuse it, you lose it.' That is what will happen to your planet. In the mess the world is, new babies won't even be born as parents aren't even proper parents anymore and the men who want to play God by cloning humans

will be punished more than they know. The earth stands accused of neglect of the highest degree. Our orders come from the highest power of all…"

While Lucy listened, she remembered she was given a form to fill in at school, but had not yet done it. Her Mum had told her to ignore it and the teacher had insisted it was a must and "for the good of the child." She also remembered that her parents had not been allowed to take photographs of her at school or at the local swimming pool before it had been closed down for good due to "health and safety violations," as it had been used for aqua aerobics and there was too much water in it. The attendant's excuse was "it was for the good of all children," but this meant that her childhood was not recorded and photographed at all in public places and the places were getting few and far between. Also, most of the British history had been wiped from her school's curriculum for strange reasons she could not comprehend. The world had gone PC mad. Frank had often said PC meant *Pathetic Cretins*, not politically correct. Most of the rules were mind boggling to say the least. No wonder poor Lucy and all the other younger children were confused.

The creature continued his speech to Lucy, who was now fascinated as the puzzle bits began to fall terrifyingly into place.

"Also, all the places you had visited with your parents and all the photos that they had been banned from taking are over here in this machine," his thoughts said to her while he was pointing to a huge glass globe. *"You can take what you need, my child. These are your memories taken away by a tiny group of people who stripped your land of worth, and made innocence a dirty word. All the special pageants you were denied and all the songs you were not allowed to sing are stored here in this ship. This is the final and only place children can be children. The words or books you could no longer read or say because of this group are all stored here too.*

"The control is like a cancer, an insidious disease that has crept in so gradually that no one has noticed. It started with just a few things, like the photographs being banned "for the good of the child" or forms being filled in at your schools, or certain decorations or pageants disallowed and so it crept through and will keep on winding its way into every aspect of the earth, until it's

totally destroyed. Of course this tiny group will argue this and say "no, no, we are doing what's best." But do not believe them, for they have a hidden agenda. Just like in Germany in 1939 and so many other times that man has misused power. Our other attempt to help the earth was thwarted when one of our kind was found, then trapped, killed by humans and placed in a huge jar in area 51 so they could study it, although it would later be denied. So earth children, beware. We also know that soon, for identification purposes, they will go further than the ID card you have now, as there will be a bar code tattooed on every person. For 'the common good' the given reason will be. But the fact is that anyone who has an ulterior motive will always bypass such things very cleverly indeed, so yet again the innocent people suffer for a small minority. Or as in the words of one of your more enlightened leaders, William Pitt, the younger, "Necessity is the plea for every infringement of human freedom. It is the argument of tyrants; it is the creed of slaves." A bit like your car insurances, they are so high, the premiums that your parents pay for the idiots that don't have any insurance, so they suffer because of a small minority

Lucy was agog; she had read the papers. Her parents were smashing and never bothered with the bans that seemed to be more and more common place; the "do not do this and do not do that; do not say this, or mention that" were all over the place. In one park in Essex there were 10 notices prohibiting things before you even stepped foot into the park! And she had read the books in secret that were not supposed to be read as they were stored in her parents' attic, *illegally of course*, but they were just kid's books; not of any harm really but banned nonetheless. Her Mum, especially, often argued with authorities that this was wrong. She remembers her Mum getting very annoyed with WE.C.U officers just after Christmas.

Why on earth can't we say singing from the same hymn sheet? This is ridiculous, she would moan. *And there is NO such thing as Ba Ba happy sheep! You are cretins of the highest order*, she would say.

But they always had the power, the power that was creeping through so slowly that it was impossible to detect so no one took any notice except the ones that saw through the concealment like Lucy and Frank's parents did.

This Lucy didn't realise, that all the things that went on in school or in the shopping malls, or at the swimming pools or Play Park, council rules were in force and had been for a while without anyone really noticing it. Now it all made sense.

"What can we do?" Asked Lucy.

"Alas, you yourself on your own cannot do anything, but you and your family can help plant a device that will make people who run your lands see sense. Common sense is something that has not been used for nearly 100 years or more in this country alone. It will be like turning on a TV of truth so everyone can watch and learn, learn and watch. We will need the assistance of Frank and Jerry. Do you think they will aid us?"

"Are you kidding? They would jump at the chance; they love getting into mischief; the more the merrier is their motto."

"Go fetch them here; do not look at the lake, as we know you have done that already, with disastrous result. Your nightmares were bad, weren't they? That's the source of power. The leaders get their control by siphoning the evil that

lies at the bottom of the lake. The lake flows past into the Thames too, which has contaminated the south of England."

"Go and fetch them, my child and bring them here. Just Joe will be wandering around chatting about his fish; he really is the 'red herring', stopping people from finding us here and watching the lake's water level and, of course, reporting to us about the earth's actions."

Lucy climbed down the ramp and out of the ship, and ran over to the boys who had been looking for Lucy.

"Where the blazes have you been?" shouted Jerry, red faced and worried.

"Look bro, no time to answer that, you two follow me, I've got something SO awesome to show you. Don't freak out, it's totally safe," she reassured them, who both had a worried look on their faces. Just Joe was wandering round the lake and smiling to himself.

When Frank, Lucy and Jerry got to the clearing, the boys let out a gasp.

"Cor! A ship!" they shouted in unison.

The blue space people greeted them, took their hands, and lead them up the ramp into the ship.

"Wow, looks just like the inside of World of Warcrafts stormwind city, my fave game of all time; music and everything," laughed Frank.

"Naaa," said Jerry. "Just looks like my dad's shed where we play model railways, blimey! It's all here too."

So they were right, thought Lucy, it's our dreams that are held here and all that is precious to us is stored here away from prying eyes.

"Children on the earth grow up so fast and are left to fend for themselves at a very early age. The food they are fed makes them behave badly and it's not their fault; they are forced to wear clothes far too old for them; thus, making them look more grown up; a childhood here in this country is only around 5 years, if that. In some countries they are married at 11 years old. By the time they become teenagers they are usually lost in themselves...it's a desperate situation; this is

why we have been observing this place. We now feel enough is enough. There are good parents and people in this world but they are getting few and far between as they get more and more controlled. The good people know who they are. The special power of the three of you is that you are all related by blood, which makes it work for us. You are also unmarred by the brainwashing because your parents are good people. I shall explain what is needed."

Frank, Lucy and Jerry waited. Lucy thought it strange that the three of them could be in the same room but see three different things! She still saw Nanna's old room and Santa sitting in the old chair smiling at her, gifts at his feet. And the boys had their favourite places too: the shed and the game. It was so cool, she thought.

"Please follow me," said the blue creature. That was the first time he ever said words out loud.

They all followed him into the back of the ship, down some stairs, and across a ramp that stretched across the ship's hull.

Jerry looked around in wonder. He saw the crystal globe and heard an immediate explanation in his head as to what it was and why it was there. In fact, information about anything any of them looked at was given to them without a word being uttered. What a brilliant use of thought. No words, just the information readily available. Jerry thought this was so cool and smiled as he entered the room where the creature was guiding them.

Inside the dome-like room the ceiling stretched on for miles. Millions of books lined the hundreds of book shelves. Photos depicting family innocence, stuffed into boxes, all banned from use, taken by the creatures to safeguard the children's memories. All taken memories would be restored if the plan worked.

The creature pointed to the crystal, as big as a tennis ball, and said that it needed to be placed into the House of Parliament's basement. Crystals would need to be placed in three other areas of the United Kingdom by other groups of three. This would be happening in capital cities all over the world. The crystal was handed over to Jerry and he was instructed to put it in his rucksack.

"All these crystals emanate a truth and common sense beam, which makes the leaders see sense, start helping instead of hindering, and the control stops. The power from the lake subsides. Only human children can do this as they are innocent in thought and deed.

"Many children around the world are ready to do the same as you; thousands of children, in fact. There are other things of which you must be aware. You should not tell your parents. No other person in authority should be told, as they would alert the security forces. They are called WE.C.U group. I understand you are familiar with them. In an instant they would take you away. "For the good of the child" they would say, but you must avoid them, as they are a strange group of people who wear red stripy, woolly socks and bobble hats. These people MUST be avoided as they can cause havoc with a stroke of a pen."

He handed each child a red box; on the box were four symbols. This, they were told, was for emergencies. If they pressed the second symbol, which looked like a backwards F they would return to the safety of the ship. If they pressed the third symbol, they would be grouped together as the three. Three was powerful, so if needed they could join and fight.

The three kids stared at the boxes and placed them carefully in their pockets.

Rome.FM Italia Strange lights have been seen over the Vatican. Sources say that it was just festive fireworks, but the underground "UFO group MeC" say it's not of this earth. The Vatican remains quiet on the subject.

- 49 - | P a g e

Chapter 5

The Medallion

The creature showed them more of the huge ship and gave them their instructions. Lucy was in charge, said the creature, as she was the youngest and most innocent in her mind. She would see the bad aura of the authorities, especially if she wore the medallion that he now placed around her neck. This would warn them about whom to trust; there would not be many of them.

When the medallion was round her neck, she saw the auras of Frank and Jerry shine bright and silver. If the auras shone red, then there would be danger, the creature informed her.

"Of course, red is the colour you would associate with danger and it is made so, for you. It is not to be taken off at all, as this has an aura of protection in the ruby that sits in the centre; this protects you all while you're doing this task. You should take the train into London; the evening train if possible, we understand how bad the trains are and that the time tables are disastrous, so go earlier than your intended time. You must be in the basement of the House of Parliament at midnight on the 29th of this month, which then it is a full moon. This helps you scout around in the dark, no other reason than the moon is Nature's torch and will protect you. You can tell your parents you are on an overnight trip to the planetarium with the scouts; this will all be arranged for you so you could travel down in relative ease."

The three walked home. As they wandered out of the forest, at the edge of the black and white, photograph-looking path, just before it went to colour again, there in the middle of the path was the mushroom basket. It was filled to the brim with mushrooms and packed with blueberries. Their alibi for the time they had been away was now set. The journey could now begin. Lucy had butterflies in her tummy. She held onto the T-shaped medallion that was round her neck. The boys were a little envious, but they had their red boxes, so that helped a little.

When they got home, the fact that they had given a full basket of mushrooms and berries to their Mum gave no rise for questioning at all.

"Aunty Sue, we had fun finding them," said Frank with a smirk.

Lucy and Jerry stifled a giggle. Their Mum was okay with just about anything; loved them very much, was hell-bent on their freedom as children, and was a "stay-at-home Mum"; something that was very rare in this world and getting rarer by the year. This was due to a whole mess of reasons; one of them was the worship of money and belongings. Everyone wanted bigger, better, and more all the time, and no one was ever happy with half measures. The shops were always full; a bit like the Whos of Whoville in Dr. Seuss's book, How the Grinch Stole Christmas. People frantically bought more and more as the Christmas season neared.

It was a week before the 29th came, so they had time to plan the trip in detail. They would be allowed to visit the ship for more information if needed. In fact, they were determined to go back. The medallion shone brightly round Lucy's neck but her Mum didn't notice. The aura round her Mum was orange, which meant she cared unreservedly for her children and family. Her dad's aura was the same, although it had a blue tinge which meant protector of the child. She felt comforted by that, but it didn't surprise her. Lucy went up to her room and left the boys playing race cars on the Xbox.

She turned on her laptop and scoured the internet for clues of what was going to happen. She wondered what the other children were like. She went onto the newspaper webs; the *Daily Mail* was her dad's favourite so she read the main articles. One of them caught her eye. It read:

> *London UK 2015AD. In the law 2708 section 4, "for the good of the child" the child will now start senior school at the age of 9, not 11, as it has been for many years. Assemblies or other groupings of people en mass will now be prohibited, all scout and guide clubs disbanded nationwide from January 2016, and a full confiscation of the camera use in public will be implemented by the end of the year, a spokesman commented. ....*

Lucy could not believe her eyes; things that she didn't think were possible had been passed by law. Children being forced into starting the big school! She herself wasn't ready for the big school! This was madness; she printed off the page and saved it to show the boys. This had to stop!

This made Lucy even more determined. Jerry had the Crystal in his backpack ready for the trip next week and she would make sure they made this trip successfully.

As promised, the letter from the scouts, albeit fake, dropped through the letter box the next morning. With even the form that every parent filled in triplicate due to health and safety regulations. "For the good of the child," of course! If a child fell or played without being supervised it would be disastrous! Woe betide you for having honest fun! That would be awful, wouldn't it? Lucy laughed when she read the forms her Mum had to fill in and she muttered to herself about the laws ruining kids childhoods, etc.

Lucy just planted a huge kiss on her Mum's cheek and was so glad she could not be brain washed. No cameras allowed either on the trip. That did not bother them as this was a fictitious trip anyway. But they had to go with the flow on this one.

They had one more week off from school for half term, then the quest they had been asked to do would be implemented on the Sunday before they went back to school. Lucy was excited and kept watching the news for hints of the other kids.

But it had been such a secret that no other groups knew about the other. They did, however, practice the red boxes and all pressed the button to get together as 3. This worked and was fun to try. Each sat in their room and pressed the button. Suddenly, they all landed in Lucy's room, and they laughed at this. This could be so much fun, but they did realise that it could well be dangerous too. They did not want their parents to get into trouble and definitely not to be taken away by the WE .C.U group.

The train heaved into the station. Late as usual, very crowded, and with broken toilets the norm, they had booked seats and politely asked the youths that had taken their seats to get up. Fortunately, they did. This was weird, because normally they would just tell you to bog off. They just looked at Lucy and got up immediately. Frank thought it was the medallion that was working some kind of magic.

They sat in their seats, most of the passengers looking stressed, and the younger generation hiding behind modern day pacifiers; iPods or mobiles clutched tightly like safety blankets in their hands. You could hear the discord round the carriage. If it was any louder it would make your ears bleed.

Frank started telling jokes, as this was his way of killing time and dispelling any nerves he might be feeling.

"Ok...where should a 500 pound alien go, Jerry?" giggled Frank.

"No idea, but you're going to tell me anyway," he laughed.

"On a diet," laughed Frank.

Lucy just groaned, "Here we go again."

With Frank's banter the journey was fun and fast, with views of crappy scenery from outside rubbish flying about the train tracks from illegal fly tipping. They reached Charring Cross Station by 10:30 pm; plenty of time to get to Westminster Station to take the underground. Lucy did notice that the passengers on the train became calm round them. As their journey progressed, the stress levels of the train passengers became non-existent. Was it the crystal or the medallion? They were about to find out in more ways than one.

They got off the train and walked towards the underground which wasn't too far. The streets were bustling with night people having fun; although gangs were also spilling out of the pubs, so they would have to be very careful. The three kids with rucksacks must have seemed really strange in this bustling city. There were many languages spoken on the streets, not any that the children recognised. Buskers played their instruments, vying for the attention and spare coppers of the passers-by. Lucy automatically put 50 pence in a guy's hat and he smiled.

"God bless you lassy," the busker said and smiled.

Lucy noticed his aura was silver. That was nice to see; in fact, there were a lot of silver auras, but some red ones too, which they avoided like the plague.

Lucy saw London full of colours. The children's colours were the saddest as they were grey which meant unhappiness, *and they were being dragged along on journeys to shops! So late at night too,* thought Lucy. London never slept. Obviously!

Frank and Jerry were laughing and joking. Frank's steady stream of stupid jokes kept them entertained while they walked the streets. The streets and buskers reminded Lucy of a song her daddy sang to her when she was younger, *"Let me take you by the hand and lead you through the streets of London."*

London had changed since she was a little girl. Now it was busy and messy and had too much traffic for her liking. Lucy being only 8 years old, the city had changed fast in just 2 years.

They went down the escalator and caught the underground tube to Westminster. They were all in high spirits as they rode the tube. Lucy was not too keen on being underground and the noise of the other trains made her ever so slightly nervous. Still with Frank and Jerry at her side, it would be okay. The medallion nestled on her breast bone under her T-shirt and the crystal was safe in the Jerry's back pack.

Suddenly, the train came to a shuddering halt and the lights dimmed.

"Please try to stay calm and stay seated; there is something on the track and this is being dealt with very fast indeed." BING BONG, then the speaker went dead.

Actually that's what the three of them guessed he had said, as the English he had spoken was with a very strange accent and it had been difficult to catch every word.

Then, after 15 nerve-racking minutes of waiting with Jerry looking impatiently at his watch, the speaker broke its silence once again.

BING BONG

"Now the debris on the track is no longer there. Please be seated properly."

And with a shudder, the train started on the journey again.

"We have 45 minutes to get our task finished. I hope this tube has no more stops," breathed Jerry.

"Ah, no worries mate, it will be fine," encouraged Frank.

ZodoFF

Svenksa dag bladet Sweden 2015. The official lists of words that are deemed unsuitable and may cause upset are being distributed to all schools around the globe. Parents are advised to teach their children so as not to cause offence. Ministries say it's "for the good of the child."All jewellery bearing any emblem is now prohibited. Protests by the parents on freedom of speech being wrapped in a cotton wool society have been ignored, an official source comments......

Chapter 6

Just like Guy Fawkes

The three walked across Saint James Park, skirting the pond, and then on towards Parliament Square. It was now, according to Jerry's watch, 11:15 pm, so time was on their side.

"Any thoughts on how we are going to get through the locked gates?" Frank asked.

"Actually," said Lucy, "our blue alien friend told me that if we placed the crystal by the railing, it melts the metal." She smiled to herself at having information that the boys did not.

As they walked over to the railing, they were stopped by a policeman.

"What are you doing here at this time of the night then, eh?" Police had zero tolerance and would arrest a person even for talking back to them. Lucy stepped forward and said,

"Good evening sir, we are just on our way to meet our parents, who are meeting us on the other side of the square."

"Well just mind how you go then, miss." And the policeman smiled.

And that was it? No moaning, or body searches, ID checks or anything? Lucy guessed it was the power of the medallion she was wearing...she hoped she could keep it after the quest.

The tall iron railings were wet due to the rain that had fallen earlier in the day; they walked around them out of the sight of the ever watchful policeman. There was no way they could climb them, so they would have to use the crystal. Frank checked to see if the coast was clear and got the crystal out of Jerry's backpack. He held the crystal against the railings and they melted like chocolate, dripping slowly down the rails, he moved the crystal up and down until the hole was big enough for them to climb through.

They walked towards the back of the House of Parliament and looked for a place to get into the building.

"Over here," whispered Lucy, pointing to a set of steps that lead down to a basement room or something.

This was a stroke of luck that they did not expect, but Lucy thought that the medallion that hung round her neck somehow kept them safe, and aided them in their quest.

At the bottom of the stairs was a metal door. There also hung a huge padlock on a chain.

"This might be the booze entrance," laughed Frank.

"This is where Mum says all the tax payers' money goes," Jerry giggled.

"Just think Frank, tons of bottles of booze lined up ready to be sold back to the people who bought it in the first place with hard earned cash!" Jerry laughed.

"My dad would say, pity it's not petrol instead! This country alone has the highest fuel tax in the world."

They all laughed, but somehow knew that their parents' moaning had legitimate arguments behind it. And they respected their parents for that. They could not be brainwashed like most parents. This is why the three children were chosen for this task. And all over the world 3 special children would be in all the capital cities, children of different colour skin, different races, different beliefs, but with one goal: to be free, to think with total freedom and to be safe in the world. Freedom has a price, say some people, but that is that people usually go to war. Freedom should be there for anyone to use at will. No negotiating should be necessary. It should not matter what you look like; we are all the same under the skin. Only our attitudes make us different. And that's sad; so very, very sad.

They knew that when the crystal was in place they had to use the red boxes to get to the ship for stage 2. They had no idea what stage 2 was; but they didn't care; they knew this was the world's only chance to get back on track before it was completely and irreversibly ruined.

The crystal was held up over the huge chain and padlock and they watched the metal melt like cheese in a microwave.

"Awesome," beamed Frank. He started out light-heartedly with a joke. "Oh yes...a tax auditor got held up by a robber, who said, 'give me all your money.' The tax man, very shook up, said 'but I'm a tax man; you can't do this!!!' So the robber held the gun to him again and said, 'Okay, mate, give me MY money back then."

Frank laughed his head off. Lucy just made a tutting sound at him and Jerry giggled and pushed open the big door. The three of them looked around, not sure where to head off. But Lucy's medallion started to beep, and the ruby was glowing. As they walked down a long corridor, it was eerily quiet. Frank checked his watch, 10 minutes to find the cellar. They followed the beeps and when they were really strong, they were near another set of steps that lead down even further.

"This must be the way; come on guys hurry," encouraged Lucy.

They walked down the stone steps, and pushed open the wooden door at the bottom.

"This is the place, I just know it is!" cried Lucy.

Frank and Jerry took steps to find a good place for the crystal to lay undetected, and found a nice place behind some barrels and boxes that were so dusty, Guy Fawkes must have left them there when he tried to blow the place up back in 1605. They thought this was as good a place as any.

Gently, they laid the crystal dead on midnight. As soon as they did, it started to pulse, alarming them slightly.

The pulse was vibrating through the House of Parliament. They had been instructed to stay there for 10 minutes before transporting back to the ship.

They sat on the dirty floor cross-legged, and Jerry got out some sandwiches his Mum had made and some juice for them all. So a mini, down the dusty cellar, picnic was in force.

"I think before we leave here, we must shut all the doors again so as not to arouse suspicion," Lucy said, and she handed the newspaper printout

ZodoFF

she had gotten off the internet to the boys to read. Frank nearly choked on his sandwich.

"They can get knotted if they think they will ban my camera out in public! Who are these morons? Who do they think they are kidding? 'For the good of the child?'" He mimicked. "My backside." Frank was fuming. Jerry was no better.

"My camera is in my pocket all the time! I'm always taking shots! What are they going to do, this WE.C.U group, start strip searching us at schools? Confiscate anything they like? Well, they can go to planet ZodoFF, for all I care," fumed Jerry.

"Okay you two, get off your soap boxes, what we are doing here will hopefully put a stop to all this nonsense and bring this country back to being the great place it used to be to live in." Lucy beamed a great smile and chomped on her sandwich.

After the ten minutes were up, the three of them shut and checked the doors they had opened and pressed their backwards F symbol to get to the ship. They held hands as they did, not sure what would happen to them, but feeling safer that way.

Africa news beat 2015. More and more boys as young as 6 are being kidnapped and taken into rebel armies, despite Amnesty International stepping up its support. "This seems like a very long tunnel with no light at the end," comments AI spokesman.

Chapter 7

Ground Control to Major Tom

The three children appeared on the floor of the glass dome in the main hull of the ship. The smiling aliens surrounded them, knowing the children had succeeded in the first part of the quest.

The communication thus followed, while the David Bowie song "Major Tom" was played through invisible speakers throughout the ship. The aliens smiled at Frank, as they knew this was his dad's favourite song. Always accommodating the little earth children.

"At precisely midnight all over the world, the chosen children of the world completed the task of righting the wrongs of the earth and putting back common sense and truth. The task is still not complete; however, as they will need to implant several smaller crystals everywhere they go, into schools and other places where children

are in a controlled environment. This task will be easier for you as only you can see the crystals. The crystals are passed along with a smile; when you smile, you activate the crystal force and it's transferred over to the one you smiled at. Once that person has the transfer, it spreads, so if that person smiles at another, the force is activated and so it goes on, spreading, undetected, and very infectious. This causes happiness and a tranquil spirit, something that has been lacking in the entire world for centuries."

The three children knew that the task was appreciated and that the fun was only just beginning. Just smiling was all it took. Just a tiny movement? It would be as simple as a smile! It took less energy to smile than it did to frown, so this was "easy peasy lemon squeezy!" They all had this same thought as a broad smile came across their lips.

The boys were given a special watch similar to Lucy's medallion, but very boyish in appearance. It, too, would not be detected by anyone and would protect them in their future quest, should there be any. They all hoped there would be, especially if the earth had to be evacuated, or whatever the plans were.

Still listening to the music playing, the "Blues Crew" (which they had been silently nicknamed by Frank) had offered the children a trip to their world after they completed the task. Their world was called Neveh, and it was a million light years away from earth.

This task would take 4 weeks to cover the area in which they lived. Then they would be given an aid to travel in a special pair of travel pants. When these were put on you could say "travel pants take me to where I want to go," and then you would go to that place.

This was most exciting for the three, as they just loved to travel. At least they did not have to go through airports, as they were a hyped-up, long queuing mass of total confusion. All customers were treated like cattle at a market being herded through, with no respect for you or your belongings, as they were thrown onto a conveyor belt to be checked by someone who obviously hadn't a clue about working with humans! Lucy smiled to herself with a glint in her eye as she had a vision of the boys wearing big girl's knickers in which to travel around. She laughed out loud and the boys glared, even though they had no idea what she was laughing at. They guessed it would be something at their expense!

They stayed on the ship and then were asked to move up a level because the aliens had something to show them. One of the blue creatures flicked a switch and thousands of TVs lit up along the walls of this glass-domed room.

All of the countries from all over the world flashed into view... the screens showed wars, children being hurt, bullies, avarice, death, destruction of the planet, forests burning, and rules being read to scared communities. TV screens flashed with scenes of books being burnt in huge piles as big as mountains round the world's cities. Bad parenting, neglected children on streets fending for themselves. Phone tapping, internet spying was rife in towns and cities, death squads roamed the streets and took life without a thought. And the group WE.C.U causing havoc for innocent families around the globe, not using forethought or common sense; it was endless.

The three stood there, jaws dropped at all the pictures flashing in front of them. It was impossible to comprehend the sheer wanton stupidity of man. What must the Blues Crew think of them? They got their answer.

We know what you are thinking, earth children; this is not your fault. Many times efforts have been made to curb your violent world. Well over 2000 years ago a special person came to help, but he was killed. Just like all other attempts were thrown away. But this time we arrive in force. And the use of the power of 3 will be stronger. On our planet there is no such thing as violence or wars and the young and old are cared for as they should be. No animals like the red panda or the white tiger face extinction like they do on your earth. All animals are special. Respect reigns high on our planet. It does not at all on yours; humans revel in ridiculing each other through media or bullying one another. It's just not cool to be cruel. So this is your chance to help. Now off you travel and good luck with your Crystal spreading." The creature walked towards them gracefully and smiled, pointing to the ships exit.

The three children walked out from the ship and into the forest. None of them broke the silence that had enveloped them. It was indeed time to get home and to get this sorted. This had

to be done in utmost secrecy without WE.C.U catching them!

Daily Mail UK. December 2015 as all school trips, field trips and most other forms of recreational trips have been banned for some time. The ministry now says in spite of insurance premiums getting so high and destroying any form of school trips, it was still in the best interest of the children; "health and safety regulations are a must." School teacher's protest, but the "insurance robbers" insist that the premiums paid for a simple trip to a park are honest and unavoidable.

Chapter 8

Rule Weary!

The time spent in the ship was so awesome for the three children. It was because of their special upbringing, the simple fact that their parents had enough common sense to bring the children up with free and open minds. Very rare these days, of course, but that's why these children were chosen in the first place. Lucy was a special girl; being only 8 years old and still innocent in deed and thought made her powerful in this world. More than she would realise. Poor Frank really got on his soap box when he got started. Just like his aunty really, he hated injustice and stupid people, and often wondered why the world was full of them! He had often thought they could all pop off to the planet ZodoFF, which was a great place for stupid people; maybe the *Blues Crew* could siphon them up!

The silence broke...

"See you tomorrow, you two." smiled Frank.

"Remember, don't get caught with that camera, Frankie boy," Jerry laughed.

"Well, you know which planet they can travel to, eh!!!" Frank laughed out loud.

Jerry was glad to have a cousin like Frank. He played a lot of games with him. Frank was an only child and Jerry was just as important to Frank too, he having no siblings to rely on.

"See you later in the morning; I have stuff to do in the early part of the morning, okay?"

Frank laughed and headed for home, which was not far from Jerry's and Lucy's house. They were lucky they lived near the open fields with a forest not too far away from them, as this served as a good camouflage when they went out exploring. They could sneak out undetected as it was forbidden to play unaccompanied. The "non-authorized play time" rule was in force in case anyone got hurt. So this was easier for them. Their parents had always scoffed at the pathetic health and safety council rules that stopped everyone having fun. If you were even caught littering you would be fined heavily. But in truth, landfill after landfill was filled with all the carefully recycled paper from citizens, without a care for the environment, usually shipped to foreign lands out of the way. So, it was a waste of time and money spent on microchip bins and boxes. "A rule for them and a rule for us" as per usual, which is what everyone thought of them...the world was dying. We were separate from nature with not a care or thought for it. There was always something that was being banned or a rule to be implemented for one thing or another, usually a stupid rule that made no sense whatsoever.

North Korea news beat. 2015 All borders will now be closed. All exit visas now prohibited. Those who are caught trying to escape via the country side to the south will be shot on sight. The 17th nuclear test was implemented September without warning. No comment was offered by the Korean government.

Chapter 9

The Wise and the Wary

The school start was the following Monday so all three got themselves organised for the task ahead.

Lucy had been thinking about the crystal force to get over to the kids in school, and to the teachers. She knew the teachers were just as fed up as they were; the rules changed so much in school, that even the teachers were confused.

School began as normal, well nearly normal; assembly was banned, and Lucy's school was one of the last schools to have an assembly, with hymns and the Lord's Prayer, etc., like her Mum used to tell her they had way back in the *olden days*.

There was one teacher called Mrs. Wilson, always so angry, so Lucy made her way through the corridor to her room and knocked on the door.

"Yessss," the harsh voice behind the door sounded.

"Morning, Miss," smiled Lucy as she stood in the doorway and felt the crystals release; she crossed her fingers behind her back.

Mrs. Wilson glared, hiccupped, and said "Well, good morning Lucy, my dear."

That was a first! She never ever said 'my dear.' Wow it works? She thought. *This is going to be FUN!* She then walked off to class registration, if that hadn't been banned too!

She wondered how Frank and Jerry were getting on at the big school, as their school was just full of angry, iPod-wearing teens with a grudge against the world.

She went to class and smiled at everyone that was grumpy or who looked miserable. It was remarkable how everyone reacted; even at lunch time when all the kids had their E numbers for lunch, except Lucy, of course. She had school dinners which were great, mashed potatoes and meatballs. She couldn't understand why the kids brought rubbish to school to eat. Her Mum loved cooking and hardly ever used tinned food. She always used fresh ingredients.

In her maths lesson, Lucy sat quietly and listened to the teacher Mr. Spicer. She liked him and never messed about in his classes like some of the other kids did. She had face ache because of smiling at everyone and would be glad when this day was over. She wondered how long this would take to get everyone happy and sorted.

At the end of final lesson the bell rang, shrill and noisy mixed with the kids footsteps clattering on the iron steps in the hallways connecting the classes. She walked outside into the October weather, grey and dull; the sunshine had long gone and hid itself behind a whopping great big cloud that threatened rain.

As always, her Mum was there to meet her outside the school gates. Parents were not allowed into the school at all, even if your own child hurt him or herself. A stupid rule that her Mum ignored when Lucy had fallen last spring and no one came because the teacher did not have the authority to touch Lucy. Her Mum had practically vaulted over the gates to get to her, ranting at the teacher as she took hold of Lucy and took her home. It wasn't the teacher's fault, per se; it was the WE.C.U group's fault; but it still made her Mum angry at how they just did what the rules said and did not use any common sense at all.

"How was your day, Luce?" her Mum asked and smiled as she took her hand.

"Fine," was all she said...knowing she was not very good at telling fibs, so best to say little for safety's sake.

As they turned the corner, they saw the familiar car parked outside their house with WE.C.U in red letters on the side of the VW.

"What in the blazes do they want?" Lucy's Mum seethed.

Lucy started shaking, and wondered if they had found out what she and the boys were up too. Would they go to juvenile hall?

The two women, in their distinctive hand-knitted, boil washed, woolly tights with blue bobble hats to match, and long afghan coats, looking like 70's rejects, stood beside their car waiting for them to arrive. The women smiled at

Lucy and her Mum as if they had known them all their lives.

Lucy's Mum huffed and tutted as they got closer and closer to them.

"And what can I do you for, ladies?" she smirked.

"Well, good afternoon dear; we just would like a word or two with you about your son in school today. All for the good of the child, I might add." The smarmy WE.C.U rep smiled that awful smile that let you know you would have to sign release forms or some other worthless, time-consuming piece of garbage to keep them off your back.

Lucy's Mum went into her garden down the path and opened the door; the two bobble-hat clad women looked around suspiciously at the house, the door, the windows, and everything they could lay their eyes on, seemingly, they thought, without being noticed!

You think?!!!

"Would you like a cup of tea?" Lucy's Mum asked through gritted teeth.

"Oh yes, that would be lovely," they replied in unison as if they were joined at the vocal cords.

Lucy watched as the two women went into the living room and sat on the sofa, waiting for their tea and waiting to explain the incident from Jerry's day at school.

Lucy was worried that they had found out, but thought they were too dumb to realise the significance of the quest that she and the boys had undertaken. She smiled to herself as she watched the two women sitting, eyes darting round the room like bats. They could not see her while she sat halfway up the stairs, staring through the wooden stair rails.

When the tea pot, biscuits and tea cups were laid on the tray on the coffee table in front of the woolly sock brigade (Lucy's Mum's nickname for them), they began to speak.

"Now as we said before, Mrs. Maidstone, your son, Jerry, had been acting strange in school today, together with his older cousin Frank. Now we don't mind children using their imagination, but this was rather a scare mongering that frightened the teachers somewhat." The shorter of the two smiled then continued.

"This morning we had a report from our track officer that Jerry was somewhat evasive when asked to explain why he went around smiling at everyone in school, including caretakers, etc. This caused consternation and we felt we must investigate the matter."

Lucy's Mum nearly choked on her biscuit. "What?"

They stammered and looked at her.

"You come here to tell me that my son is behaving strangely by SMILING?"

"Well, it's not that simple," the women said.

"Not that simple? Let me tell you this, lady; if my son is smiling then it's a good thing isn't it? Especially in that school full of your pathetic spies! Whether he smiles at everyone or just one person is none of your business; geesh, you really take the biscuit, you come here with your stupid rules, saying we can't do this or that. NOW you say he's smiling too much; next minute you'll be accusing him of breathing in the wrong manner."

They sat there legs crossed-crinkled, woolly socked clad legs, and bobble hats wobbling through fear of being talked back to by this irate parent.

"Well, we think you should talk to him," they suggested.

By now Lucy's Mum was red in the face and felt like slapping their stupid faces off them, but she was wise and kept her hands in her apron pockets.

"Well, I will talk to him, as I've always talked to my children, to express themselves to live and to believe in themselves in any way they wish. So might I make a teeny weensy suggestion that you do not darken my doorstep with these pathetic accusations again?"

"Oh yes, and before I forget. Lucy will not be filling in any forms at school without our knowledge. NOT because of your say so. Got it?"

She shifted her stance and took her hands out of her apron pocket to point at the door.

The women hurried from the sofa, mumbled something incoherent, and left as fast as a dog that's smelt a sausage. This group of people were never good with parental confrontation, as it was easy to use rules and scaremongering tactics via letters and passing new laws through via the ministry.

Lucy's Mum smiled as they went out the door. She remembered the tale of her dear friend who had been a foster-care giver for over 80 children, and the council had struck her off due to the teenager in her care changing her faith. This was the moronic type of thing she hated with regards to the councils and ministries that had a about as much common sense as a gnat! No offence to the gnat, she would add. They never seemed to do any good with the rules...Lucy's Mum firmly believed that everyone could live side by side, harmony reigning full swing without the constant interference from first class idiots.

Lucy's Mum was a very rare mum these days; one, because she was a stay-at-home Mum; this was unheard of, as all parents were at work and the kids were latch key kids from the age of 8, or at some form of club or other after school. The second was that she was married, which was also unheard of, as people couldn't be bothered. The fact that people chose not to was because of the extortionate rates these so-called wedding planners charged, which just knocked people out of the "let's get married" race. So it was a no-win situation. Half of the kid's mums were only teenagers anyway.

Reuters October 2015. According to UK Gove rule, item 6652 has now been moved forward for the December festive season; under no circumstances must you use the word Christmas in conversation, and it will now be known as "winterdom." This is a follow on from Easter being prohibited last spring. Many groups are protesting, but it falls on deaf ears...........

Chapter 10

All Snuck Up!

Frank, Jerry and Lucy decided it was best if they snuck back to the ship at the weekend, if they could; otherwise, they would use the travel pants to get there unseen. They were a bit wary about using the pants and had fits of giggles trying to put them on. Frank had nearly wet himself on the floor because he was laughing so much at Jerry's big knickers over his jeans. Frank had said Jerry looked like a reject Superman. They knew school inspectors could be trouble for them if they got caught; especially if the (woolly sock brigade) WE.C.U got news of any weird behaviour happening. But smiling! Come on! What were they thinking about? This had gone too far and Lucy's Mum was out for an argument; she loathed anything that conveyed rules and stupid restrictions and often had gotten on her "soap box" about it.

On Friday evening, after tea, the three got together and snuck out into the back garden. Obviously, their Mum knew that they were out playing, but it wasn't her they were sneaking away from. After the visit by the weird women of WE.C.U, the ministry had a car parked not far from the house and was obviously watching. This was happening more and more across the UK and also stretched over Europe and further. Even the police had set up spy posts to spy on people they thought to be undesirables, connected with anything they did not agree with, however small. All e-mails in every household were scanned by a huge data base in London before you actually received it in your mailbox. Nothing was private anymore and the governments all over the world tightened their grips over everyone. Nothing was safe. Not even bank accounts. Tax was now always deducted immediately. It was squandered on anything the ministry wished to spend it on. You had no say in the matter. Lucy's father at one time had refused to pay before it became a compulsory deduction. He had insisted that the money was used to line the pockets of fat cat wealthy ministers and bankers with no thought of the people that lived in the country and worked hard for every penny they earned just to have it practically stolen from your account before you had the chance to move it. Frank's dad always said, "The mattress was the only safe bank in the world."

When they ran through the forest, they felt relieved and hoped that the ship was still there.

"I hope we were not followed," Lucy said in a worried tone.

"Don't worry, they are too stupid for that," one of the boys said and they laughed and took Lucy by the hand and ran towards the ship's lights. Running to the ship gave them a buzz and was far more fun than travel pants!

Once there, the Blues Crew came to greet them and seemed to know all that had gone on at school. These super intelligent beings were more surprising every time they met them.

"Greetings, I see the power of 3 is working well; we are very pleased with the results so far."

The lights around the ship shone brightly as the children walked up the gang plank of the ship, the familiar tune of the nightingale sang in Berkley square could be heard by Lucy; the familiar surroundings that the three children had witnessed the first time in the ship were also the same. They looked around them and marvelled at the beauty of the huge Crystal in the centre of the ship. It glowed as huge amounts of information stored there became copious.

We are sorry for the trouble you have been in with the ministries that control your country; they have not yet learned what freedom is and so will continue to be suspicious of anything until this whole mess is sorted.

We would like to take you on a trip to Neveh, if you so desire it. This will help make you stronger and help you learn something of our kind. And most importantly, it's safe there, as we have learned that things have just escalated and are in need of some serious attention.

In unison, the boys said, "WHAT, you kidding??? Of course! Blimey! What a question."

The Blues Crew smiled.

Chapter 11

Neveh, Neveh Land

As the ship ascended into the sky, the children held each other by the hands; they were worried, but did feel safe with the Blues Crew. The world almost immediately became a blue speck on a never ending, star-laden sky highway.

They stared out of the space ship windows, watching everything whoosh past them in seconds. The stars became huge lights cascading over the ship; the wormholes they shot into felt like they were on a roller coaster ride in Disneyworld; the astral belts that shot past them were immense and the depth of colour was purely breathtaking. It all happened so fast that they held their breath while watching.

All of a sudden, the whooshing sound decreased and the ship hovered over the most beautiful light-laden city they had ever seen; all colours of the rainbow shone like stars from heaven itself. Huge towers stretched up to the skyway in massive crystal structures of immense beauty. Field after field of children playing, the melodious sound of children's laughter could be heard everywhere, although the children could not be seen as they were still tiny specks. The three of them had felt a feeling of *de jà vu*, as if they had been here and seen all of this before in a time way back and long forgotten in their minds. But that was impossible...wasn't it?

Their noses were pressed up against the window of the ship as it entered the dock. The music still played in Lucy's ear; she felt an overwhelming sense of happiness and security-she had never felt before in her short life. Frank and Jerry looked in amazement as the ship's hull swung into position and docked perfectly. The almost silent hiss of the engines cooling and the great hatch opening, ready for the 3 to venture out onto the gang plank, was more than poor Lucy could stand. The excitement was so great, she could not stop smiling, the biggest Cheshire cat smile EVER!

It seemed strange to Lucy that the Blues Crew spoke uttering no syllables at all, but she heard every word of what they said in a voice that was familiar to her, although she could not put her finger on where she had heard it. She knew the

Blues Crew, knew that Frank had nicknamed them this, but they did not seem to mind; in fact, they were an immensely kind race of beings.

The 3 children were led out down the ship's gang plank and out into the open air; the air was so fresh and the smells of flowers and trees were mesmerising. Children were running about in fresh air and they could breathe without coughing. They all looked happy, well fed and content, parents cooing round them with so much love. Still no words were spoken, but the never-ending bond of parent and child was wonderful to see. Even though their parents were one of the few left that nurtured and cared in the "old fashioned" way, with a Mum at home, etc., it still was amazing to see all this. Wherever they walked on these spotless streets with funny shaped houses row upon row, no fighting, no wars, no street gangs, no stupid rules, no hunger, no bullying and no nothing! Just everyone getting along, living life as it should be. The 3 were awestruck. This reminded Lucy of the film The Wizard of Oz, when Dorothy stepped onto the yellow brick road.

Lucy went to touch a huge, red, bulbous flower on the side of the streets; it burst into a thousand tiny seeds, filling the air with scents of three different kinds of blooms floating up above her so she could touch each one like a snowflake.

Jerry and Frank walked down this strange street in this strange world; a world that seemed to run parallel with earth but, in far better shape and the beings in much better humour. But then, no wars raged, and bullying of how people looked or spoke or what colour they were did not occur and did not matter here. Life was as perfect as perfect could be imagined. The vehicles were hovering just above ground; no exhaust fumes could be smelt or seen. All of this was working in perfect harmony with the nature that surrounded it. The Blues Crew who was guiding them through this city pointed to the statue in front of them.

This, precious children, is the Statue of Human Guidance. This was here when we inhabited this wonderful land many thousands of years ago. There are three points to the statue, three rubies fill these places and have guided us for centuries. On earth there was one of these very statues but alas, greed and avarice reigned high on your planet and it was pillaged and destroyed as fast as a wink of an eye with no thought to your history or future. Several times help has been sent to try and turn the heads of you humans into respectable good people, but each time someone was sent, it ended in their death and more horrific fighting than ever before. Humans never learn; they are like small children living in a big sand pit; they fight over material things that cannot possibly be taken with you once you pass on. You are capable of such wondrous things and of such horrific nightmares! Humans pick on each other in the most insensitive ways. You kill each other over silly things; even the games you play are too severe and end in mindless violence. To what end, we ask? None is the answer. It's not cool to be cruel. The good that are left on earth are being demoralized and are in fear of retaliation from one another. Hate is very toxic.

The blue creature with its strange looks and kind manner was, of course, right. Lucy, Frank, and Jerry knew it and were pleased that the earth might just get help again and this time maybe it could work. The Crystal they had planted seemed to be working, but oh, so flipping slowly! But things come to those who are patient; this they knew; their parents had taught them well. This is why they had been chosen; this is why this would work. Hundreds of children from all over the world would be doing the very same thing...

The Blues Crew guided them into a huge mass of red carpet; it said welcome on it, in their language, of course, but who ever looked at it read it as their own language. In the distance, hordes of earth children gathered together on the mat, smiling at each other. All of different faiths, creeds, colours and countries moulded together in one huge happy mass, they greeted each other and understood one another; language was not a barrier here. The one common bond was peace and the ability to look beyond the skin that they were in. It was like the tower of Babel in reverse, a truly spectacular sight to see.

Lucy looked around her, saw a child sat in the middle of the vast welcoming mat, and went to talk to her. The colours of their skin were very different indeed. Lucy with her sun bleached hair from playing out a lot, and the little girl as dark as chocolate with an enormous white toothed smile, they greeted one another.

"My name is Lucy," she gestured and held out her hand.

"Mine is Hanan. I'm from Jordan."

"Wow, that's so cool; I'm from England, very pleased to meet you, Hanan. What a lovely, interesting name you have there."

Lucy stretched out her hand to shake it, and Hanan just gave her a hug.

This place was awesome; she felt so safe, so protected and SO happy, meeting all these children with the same quest as she had the very same goal as she. She couldn't wait to see if all their hard work had or, in fact, would pay off. The throng of children stretched far across the square, where they had all melded into one huge mass of children, laughing, gay and happy. The boys had wandered off to another group of boys about the same age as them, obviously having as much fun as herself.

"The name's Frank," he held out his hand and shook the young lad's hand with gusto.

The boy smiled and said, "My name is Hevel. I come from Israel."

"Wow, that's so cool, I've never been there," and they sat down on the mat and chatted away.

All the kids chatted away to each other, talking as if they had been friends for years. If adults had acted like these kids, the world would have been a far better place to live in and no wars or stupid acts of insane, moronic violence would ever be carried out on each other. But alas, this was not to be and this is why the children were all standing here in this beautiful place. The colours of the children were like shades of chocolate, white, light brown, cocoa, mocha and dark, so beautiful, so rich, so innocent. Like chocolate, it didn't matter what colour it was; it was chocolate. They are human children. No difference whatsoever; it is attitude that makes us different from one another.

In the back of every child's mind that day was the question of whether they would have to go back to earth. Being such a mixed up, brainless planet, ruled by greedy, back stabbing fools.

Afghanistan news beat 2015. All girls caught wearing western clothes under their burka will be beaten and sent home. Ministers say it's for the "good of the child." No protests were made and all demonstrations have been prohibited.

Chapter 12

Switcheroo

Once a hologram of every child that had visited Neveh was placed on earth, the Blues Crew set to work on the earth's people that were left. No one would know of the body switch; only the children themselves. This was to keep them safe. If the earth had to be emptied, they would have a "starter" pack like Noah did with his 3 sons and their wives during the floods to rebuild the earth's population. Hopefully, the children would be taught to use common sense and live by the rules that had been used many thousands of years ago. To aid the deception of the Blues Crew, all the hologram children acted as they would in any circumstance. The children found it highly amusing that copies were made of them; if the earth was destroyed the parents of each child would be taken to safety, as that was the wish of the children. Frank shouted to the Blues Crew before they left for earth that the rest of the humans could go to planet ZodoFF, and they all laughed. Hanan just smiled; she knew it would be a difficult task ahead. She had been chatting to another girl called Miriam, who lived in Afghanistan and was terrorised by a bad group of people. She had been banned from school, and life was not happy at all. It took all her courage and wit to get the Crystal placed in the ministry building in Kabul with her two brothers to help her. A very dangerous task it was, and would have resulted in capture and a beating, but for the quick wittedness of her two brothers who helped save the day, and her skin! The story had been the same with every child, stretching from Albania to Zagreb, Australia to Zimbabwe reaching every city on the earth's surface. No desert or mountain, sea breadth or valley was without trouble.

Trouble finds people very quickly; it's a disease, easily contracted and spreads like a bush fire with no mercy whatsoever. Creeping in from behind, if you accept it then you want it, it's as simple as that. After all, you can use the word NO.

The teachers in the schools all over the world, the parents of the children all over the globe had not the slightest inkling of the switch. Every hologram child went about its school day, play time and even getting punished; all the holograms were so exact in the copy that nothing made the difference at all. It was as if the children had never left.

The Blues Crew went about the business getting the data they needed to see if the crystals had worked. In the major cities around the globe, some had and some needed extra help. This was such a major task, as trying to change the human mind from bad habits to good ones was very difficult indeed.

The forest near Jerry's and Lucy's home was the same, although no other child ventured there; not even the holograms in case of detection, which was good as the ship was still parked in the same area. Joe was always ever on the lookout for strangers to veer them away from the ship if the need arose. The fact that the path beyond the ship changed everything into black and white was usually enough to deter the sceptical adventurer away; only the children would see it as fun; the adults usually analyse everything. The WE.C.U group was getting more and more powerful; they now had the power to search homes, remove children from families of insubordinates, and one member was now placed in every school. All for "the good of the child," of course!

After months of work on earth, no amount of coaxing or crystals seemed to be powerful enough to rid the earth of the mindless violence and the power-mad people ruling it. The animals, many extinct, now just stood as a taxidermist model in museums; many children had never seen a tiger, as they had disappeared many years ago. Plants destroyed that would have cured cancer, gone through logging and deforestation. The giant panda is also extinct through greed. Deforesting took many birds' and animals' homes. Apes and gorillas long gone....their memory fades. The only time you would see them would be in an old National Geographic magazine.

The time had now come...

Everything was in place...

This was the end for all this and there was no turning back, the human beings were incapable of managing this earth that was loaned to them thousands of years ago. As the last grains of sand ran out of the hour glass, the Blues Crews in every ship all over the world got ready. All dear relatives and parents were "globed," which was like a snow globe but the size for a human being. They would be safe in there until this battle was over. All elderly were globed too, for safekeeping until the last remaining Trouble makers was gone from the earth...

This would be a far easier task than the crystal method, but they had to try one more time, in case...you never know, do you?

One flick of a switch...that was it...over...no going back. The badness on its way out...

It had certainly "left the building."

Chapter 13

Seems Like Yesterday!

When the mist cleared, millions of "human globes" opened and the people walked out, the elderly feeling stronger, the sick being healed, all the children delivered safely back to the earth, with their families.

Jerry, Frank, and Lucy walked through the door, their parents smiling at them.

Halfway across the world, Hanan walked into her parent's apartment with her siblings following her; they all smiled...

Miriam walked free down the street in a pretty pink summer dress, everyone smiling, her parents hugging her, children playing football in the street, a sight she had not seen for so long.

Hevel, walking towards a new beginning, his friend Mustapha who lived on the other side of the boarder in Gaza could now walk over to him. No more entry permits, just peace and tranquillity, play, laughter and fun. All good!

This was the same story reflected in every child's eyes; their dreams of total world peace had come to fruition... It started with a tiny droplet of discontent within a child's dream, a child not believing in the world they lived in, the only dream was to become a celebrity or a footballer, which usually ended in disaster. No reality in their dreams, just unreachable aims and hard for the child to understand, goals set too high for the child to reach, making them sad. Children leaving school, unable to read and write, forced into a gray mass of a school environment where they were ignored, as there were too many children attending in the first place. Not the fault of the teachers, just the ministry forcing too much on them.

Children should never be sad. NEVER!

Never stop believing, and have total faith in one's self.

Epilogue

Just in case you are all wondering what happened to all the humans that attempted to destroy this beautiful earth of yours...

In the honour of Frank's made up planet, the Blues Crew sent them all to ZodoFF to fight it out for themselves. After they were all siphoned up, each one was implanted with a seed, the size of a grain of rice. This would grow in their heads until they were mature enough and common sense was realised. Then they would be returned, one by one, if it worked. If not, they would stay put, of course. I will leave that up to your own imagination as to who was siphoned up and who wasn't! ZodoFF had been formed from an old star deep in the galaxy with the same climate as earth, one of many you see. The humans were all shifted so fast and placed on this planet before they could say, "whatever!" Those that would stay on the planet were placed in huge "snow globes" for protection, so they were not "vacuumed up" to ZodoFF.

The Blues Crew delighted in the fact that the earth could now start again; anyone who was left was at peace with themselves and wanted peace in the world. No tyranny existed. Animals that were left would be able to reproduce in freedom. Forests thrived, birds sang. All laws were fair to everyone. Banks were honest with your money and did not steal it with bogus charges. Pensions were given fairly and not skimped on. Children, especially in the United Kingdom and the USA, were fed proper fresh food at schools by fully trained "Jamie Oliver" chefs or dinner ladies; no E-numbers used. Worldwide junk food was eradicated for good. Hospitals were spotless and matrons ruled the wards; no queuing necessary. The elderly were respected and cared for as they should be. Teenagers had places to go in the evening; parents cared for them and hugged them no matter what their ages were. Mums were at home and were there if needed by the children. Children had long, carefree childhoods. Being a mother was a career that was revered by all and not a stigma. All would be well again. The Blues Crew would keep a close eye on the earth and Lucy, being a special girl, would report back to

"Just Joe" if needed. She still had the medallion round her neck and would grow up to become someone very special indeed. In fact, everyone has that ability if they want...

The whole world *heard* the same language. Everyone was just a human being no different from the next, whether different colour, size, creed or wealth, it did not matter. It should *never* matter. Some people put their trust in the East or to the West, but in fact, you only need to look up. The Blues Crew would kindly ask us to behave and stop being so stupid, find our common sense and use it!

Silent screams have gone away.

No children's tears to dry.

The earth is at peace and full of song.

The birds again do fly.

The End...For now
So behave!
You are being watched.

ZodoFF

www.juliehodgson.com
www.cloudydaybooks.com
http://www.shamrockediting.blogspot.com